A. Culver

GLUEY

A SNAIL'S TRAVAILS

BY: VIVIAN WALSH
and J. OTTO SEIBOLD

Harcourt, Inc.
San Diego   New York   London

Requests for permission to make copies of any part of the work should be mailed to the following address: Permissions Department, Harcourt, Inc., 6277 Sea Harbor Drive, Orlando, Florida 32887-6777.

www.HarcourtBooks.com

Library of Congress Cataloging-in-Publication Data
Walsh, Vivian.
Gluey: a snail tale/Vivian Walsh; illustrated by J.otto Seibold.
p.   cm.
Summary: When Celerina the bunny moves into a new house, she doesn't realize that there is already a snail living there and that he is the "magic" that repairs anything she breaks, and even the house itself.
[1. Rabbits—Fiction.   2. Snails—Fiction.   3. Repairing—Fiction.   4. Dwellings—Fiction.]   I. Seibold, J. Otto, ill.   II. Title.
PZ7.W168945Gl   2002
[Fic]—dc21   2002000212
ISBN 0-15-216620-3

First edition
H G F E D C B A

Printed in Singapore

The illustrations in this book were done in Adobe Illustrator.
The text type was set in Joanna.
Color separations by Bright Arts Ltd., Hong Kong
Printed and bound by Tien Wah Press, Singapore
This book was printed on totally chlorine-free Nymolla Matte Art paper.
Production supervision by Sandra Grebenar and Ginger Boyer
Designed by Jeff Puda

GLUEY

This is THE STORY of GLUEY THE SNAIL.

ONCE UPON A TIME...

in a LOVELY MEADOW A STONE'S THROW away...

A bunny found an empty house and moved right in.

She was surprised the house was empty, because to her it looked like the best house in the world.

She painted her name on a sign

and hung it over the door.

Now she felt more at home.

Celerina didn't know it,
but someone else lived there, too.

It was a snail named Gluey.

Gluey noticed Celerina right away.
He thought she looked like
a nice bunny, and he was
amazed by how fast she
could move.

Gluey hoped they would
become good friends.

Gluey was a carpenter snail.

He had been working on the house for as long as
he could remember.

Houses are very important to snails.

Gluey had two—the shell on his back, which was in perfect
shape, and the bigger house that was always getting new cracks.

Gluey didn't like cracks. He fixed them.

One day Gluey was mending a corner of the house
when he heard a loud crash.
He looked inside and saw Celerina,
and she was crying.

She wiped her tears with her ears, and wailed,
"My favorite vase—destroyed!"

In his tiny snail voice, Gluey called out, "I can fix that!"
But Celerina couldn't hear him.

Snails go slow. By the time Gluey got to the vase,
the sun had set, it was nighttime,
and Celerina was sound asleep.

Carefully, Gluey began his work.
Going slow is the best way to fix a vase.

When he was done, Gluey thought the vase looked perfect.
He knew that Celerina would like it, too.

Gluey climbed back out the window,
curled up in his shell, and fell fast asleep.

Early the next morning, Celerina found her repaired vase.
"How could this be?" she wondered happily.
"Who could have fixed this for me?"

And then she thought, "Maybe it was magic."
She ran off to tell the other animals and was gone
before Gluey woke up.

Celerina loved her house.
Anytime she broke something, all she had to do was go to sleep, and then the next morning she would find it fixed.

"My house is magic!" Celerina said to her friends. "I love it!"

She told them about the things the magic had fixed. A teapot, a teacup, a plate, her favorite vase, and even the cracks in the walls of the house itself.

The animals were not impressed. "Maybe they don't believe me," she thought.

But most of them lived in holes underground, or up in a tree, and they weren't sure what Celerina was talking about.

One day while drinking tea, Celerina had a brilliant idea.
"I'll have a party. I'll invite the animals to my house.
I'll serve toast and jam . . . and then I'll break the plate right
in front of them! Won't they be surprised when it is
magically repaired!"

Celerina started making the invitations.
On each one she drew a picture of her house,
and then painted the letters P A R T Y.

Gluey noticed that the bunny was drawing pictures
of the house over and over again.
"PARTY!" read Gluey.
He wanted to help.
"I'll make the house look its best."

PARtY
at CELERINA BUNNY'S
HOUSE
"an enchanted afternoon
of toast and jam"

The decorations went up on both the inside
and the outside of the house.

On the day of the party, Celerina was in her garden.
She looked up at her house. It made her smile.
"It's never looked better," she said to no one in particular.

"Thanks," said Gluey.

Celerina saw that a snail was speaking to her.
"What are you doing on my window?" demanded Celerina.

"Oh, I'm almost done here . . . I am Gluey."

"Gooey?" she asked. Her nose twitched. "Well, I am Celerina,
and this is my house. I am having a party today and you're
not invited."

"No, ha-ha, not Gooey. My name is Gluey, and I—"

But before Gluey could finish, Celerina plucked him
off the wall and flicked him across the meadow.

As he tumbled through the air,
Gluey tucked his head into his shell.
He hoped he would land on something soft.

He landed in the middle of an especially soft mushroom.

"Hello . . . Gluey, are you okay?" a voice asked.

"My shell doesn't feel right, but— Hey, you called me by my name." Gluey poked his head out. "Do you know me?"

"Wee do."

Indeed, Gluey had landed in the center of the Wee people's village.

The village doctor was sorry to tell Gluey that there was a small crack in his shell.

"I don't like cracks," said Gluey quietly.

"Don't worry," said the doctor. "We know shell medicine, and we can fix it."

When Gluey was feeling better, he asked the Wee people how they knew his name.

"We built your house," said the doctor.
"It was our first try and we accidentally made it too big. We were ambitious."

"You are good at fixing things, Gluey," said a little girl.

"If it wasn't for you," the doctor said, "that house would have fallen down a long time ago."

"The house . . . Celerina's party!
I have to get back!" said Gluey.

ELF - PLAN

EEEE-
YUK
YUK
Yook

But the party had already begun.

None of the animals had ever been inside a magic house before. Some of the chickens looked nervous. A swan got a funny feeling about her teacup. She decided to take it back to her nest. As she tried to sneak it into her purse, it fell and loudly broke into a hundred pieces.

"Whoops!" said the swan.

"Don't worry about that," said the lovely hostess Celerina. "Just leave it there. That teacup will be fixed, and this plate, too!" Celerina said as she smashed it on the floor.

Everyone was silent. Then all the animals smashed their cups and plates on the ground, too.

A few animals, more wild than the others, began to push. There was a loud noise, the walls shook, and then . . .

. . . the house broke into pieces.

"Not to worry," said Celerina.
"This house will be fixed. It is an overnight kind of magic.
Come back tomorrow morning and you will see."

Celerina sat all alone in her garden.
Her house looked bad.
It was going to take a lot of magic to fix things this time.
Just then she saw a snail with a bandage on its shell.

"Hey, I know you. You're Gooey!" she said.
"Do you want to watch magic fix this house?"

"Yes! I sure do," said Gluey.

As they waited, he told the bunny how he had been working
on this house for as long as he could remember, and that he
certainly couldn't fix it this time so he was really glad magic
would take care of it.

"Ohhhh . . . ," said the bunny for a long time, until she could
think of something better to say.

And then she did think of something. "Gluey, this time I'm going to fix the house for you."

She tried to push a big piece of the house back where it belonged, but it was too heavy.

Celerina told Gluey her friends were coming in the morning. "They were coming to see the house, but they will be much more excited to find out about you."

Celerina and Gluey had a lot to talk about, having lived in the same house and all.

Then tired from all her work, Celerina said, "Good night, Gluey. I can't fix this house tonight."

Gluey took one last look at the broken house and said, "I wish we could fix it."

"We can!" said the Wee people, but Gluey didn't hear them. He was already asleep.

When Gluey and Celerina woke up the next morning, they saw the most amazing thing. . . .

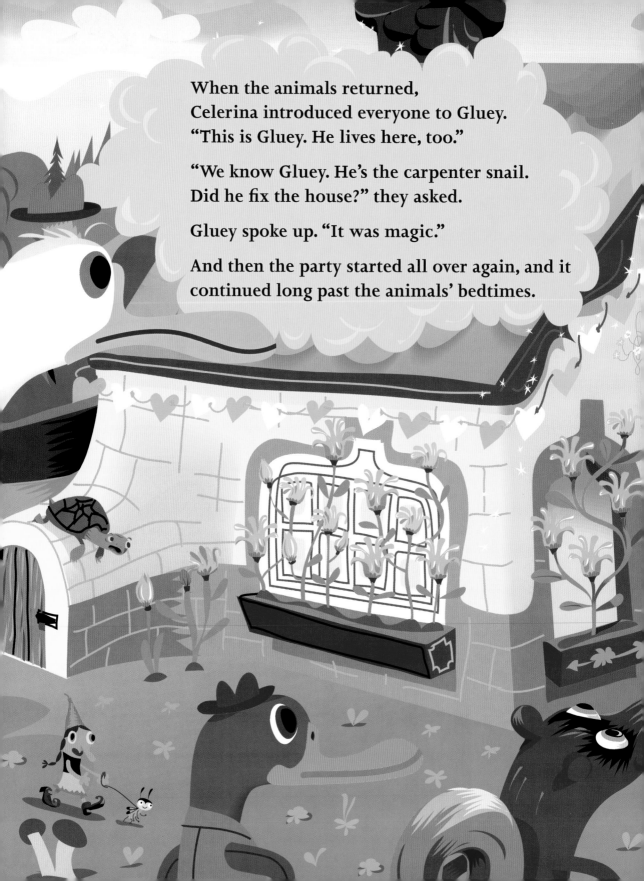

When the animals returned,
Celerina introduced everyone to Gluey.
"This is Gluey. He lives here, too."

"We know Gluey. He's the carpenter snail.
Did he fix the house?" they asked.

Gluey spoke up. "It was magic."

And then the party started all over again, and it
continued long past the animals' bedtimes.

The snail and the bunny became the dearest of friends.
They shared the house for many years.
Every now and then, Celerina would think of the night they
tried to fix the house, and she'd ask, "Did we fix it?"
And Gluey would answer, "I bet Wee did."

and they found that FRIENDSHIP was the BEST MAGIC of ALL!

THE ENd

TELL IT AGAIN!!!

in memory of
MARGARET
KILGALLEN